LUCAS'S TRICKY DAY

Looking on the Bright Side

Rajani LaRocca · *Illustrated by* **India Valle**

⌂ Charlesbridge

Lucas lives at 123 Sunshine Street with his little brother, Tommy. It's also home to their four best friends: Sophie, Oliver, Mia, and Lily.

Together they do kind deeds and spread sunshine. They're everyday heroes, and they call themselves the Sunshine Squad.

But sometimes even the cheeriest of "superheroes" needs help to brighten their day.

FREE LEMONADE

LUCAS'S
JOKES & PRANKS

♡ from
the Sunshine
Squad

Lucas loves making people laugh. It makes him feel warm and fuzzy inside.

He runs his joke shop out of the Squad's lemonade stand, and likes to surprise friends with everything from a great joke to a whoopee cushion to a squirting pen.

This morning, Lucas is on his way to the stand.
He sees his little brother, Tommy.

"Want to help me run the joke shop today?
Spread some sunshine?" asks Lucas.

FREE LEMONADE

LUCAS'S
JOKES & PRANKS

♡ from
the Sunshine
Squad

Tommy brightens. "Really? How?"

Lucas smiles. "Listen and learn."

Mia stops by the stand. She looks worried.

"What's up, Mia?" Lucas asks,
handing Mia a cup of lemonade.

"I have a soccer game this weekend.
I reeeeally need extra practice,"
says Mia.

"Hey, what's it called when a dinosaur
makes a goal?" Lucas asks.

"I don't know," Mia says.

"A dino-score!" Lucas roars.

Mia giggles as she heads to the park.

It feels good to cheer up a friend,
Lucas thinks.

Later, Lily comes to visit.

"How can I turn that frown upside down?" Lucas asks.

"I'm making a robot," Lily says. "But I can't get it to work."

"Keep tinkering! You'll get it eventually." Lucas grins. "What do you call a noble robot who likes to read?"

"I don't know," Lily says.

"Sir Read-a-bot!"

says Lucas, moving his arms like a robot.

Lily laughs. "Thanks! I'll take a walk and enjoy the sunshine, then get back to my bot."

"See, little dude? You fit the joke to the person," Lucas tells Tommy.

"Is that how you spread sunshine?" asks Tommy.

"Yup," says Lucas. "And helping friends smile makes *you* feel good too."

Lucas and Tommy's mom calls from the doorway. "Lucas, can you come inside? Henry's mom phoned about the sleepover this weekend."

"On my way!" Lucas says.

He's excited. Lucas and Henry don't see each other as often since Henry moved to a new neighborhood.

"Can Henry get here earlier on Saturday?"
says Lucas. "He's hilarious.
We'll have so much fun."

Lucas's mom frowns. "Henry's not feeling well and won't be able to sleep over. I know it was the only day we could make work this month. Sorry about that, honey."

"Oh, no!" Lucas says.
But we were going to make up our own jokes and try them out, he thinks.

Lucas goes back outside.

"Ta-da! Do you like my drawing?
Is it funny looking enough?"
Oliver asks.

"Sure," says Lucas quietly.

Lucas doesn't feel like smiling.
He's still thinking about missing
out on seeing Henry.

"Come in for lunch, Tommy," Lucas says as he plods up the steps.

"Want to play a game?" Tommy asks after lunch.

"No, I want to go be alone in my room," Lucas says as he trudges to the door. He notices that his eyes feel watery.

Lucas lies on the floor
and brings out his big joke book.
But the jokes in it don't seem funny anymore.

I bet Henry would have great ideas, Lucas thinks.
We always have the best time telling jokes together.

That afternoon, Lucas and Tommy
are at the joke shop again.

"What do you think about my
drawing now?" asks Oliver.
"I made the alien's ears bigger."

"That alien looks so
goofy," says Tommy.
"It's great!"

"Nice," says Lucas without looking.

"Are you okay, Lucas?" Oliver asks.

Lucas shrugs.

"Hey, Lucas. Got any skateboarding jokes?" Mia asks as she skids to a stop.

"Nope," Lucas says.

"What's wrong?" Mia asks.

"Nothing," Lucas replies.

Sophie comes out of the building to join them.
Now the whole Sunshine Squad is together.

"Fuzzypants would love to hear a joke," Sophie
says, stroking her pet guinea pig.

"I don't have one."
Lucas lets out a big sigh.

"Lucas, what's going on?" Lily asks.

I guess I'm sad, Lucas thinks. *Maybe I should tell them.*

"Henry can't come this weekend," says Lucas. "So now I don't feel like joking around. Sorry to let you all down."

"Oh, Lucas, I'm sorry," Mia says.
"Maybe we can cheer you up?"

"I have a joke," says Sophie.
"What's a butterfly's favorite subject
at school?"

"What?" Lucas asks.

"Mothematics!" Sophie says.

Everyone laughs, and Lucas half smiles.

"Here, have my drawing,"
Oliver says. "Oh, wait!
Let me make it even sillier.
Hand me a pen, Tommy?"

Squirt!

Splash!

"Oops!" says Tommy,
squirting Lucas with
water from the joke pen.

Lucas bursts into laughter.

"Sometimes . . . *we* can help *you* feel better!" says Mia.

"Because you always help us smile," says Lily.

"The Sunshine Squad is here for you, no matter what," says Oliver.

"Hmm," Lucas says. "I know what I can do! See you all later, okay?"

Before dinnertime, Lucas returns to the Squad.

"How're you doing, Lucas?" Sophie asks.

"Feeling sunshiny," Lucas says. "I figured Henry was sad too. So I called and told him jokes over the phone! Even though he can't come visit, we still got to hang out."

"You sure look happy!" exclaims Tommy.

"It's because of all of you . . . and the squirting pen!" Lucas chuckles. "Everyone helped me see the bright side."

"And I've got a new joke!" says Lucas. "Knock knock."

"Who's there?" Tommy asks.

"Figs."

"Figs who?"

"Figs the doorbell. I've been knocking forever!" says Lucas.

Everyone laughs, and Lucas laughs loudest of all.

The Gift of Friendship

About two weeks before my tenth birthday, I fell while I was Rollerblading and broke my wrist. I had been planning on having my birthday party at a roller rink, and now I wouldn't even be able to skate at my own party! But because we had sent out the invitations and everything was already planned, we still had to have the party at the roller rink anyway.

On the day of my party, I was standing by the front door of the roller rink greeting my friends while they came in. When one of my friends, Sarah, came in the door, I noticed that she was limping. Sarah told me that she had hurt her leg, and that her parents had told her that she could come to my party anyway if she just took it easy and only skated around the rink one time.

Sarah didn't even skate once during the whole party. All of my other friends were busy, having a great time skating—but Sarah stayed with me the

whole time. We talked about all kinds of stuff: school, our teachers, what boys we like and who we think is cute—and we laughed our heads off. Because of Sarah, my party was a lot more fun than I thought it was going to be.

A few weeks later, I saw Sarah's mom at the store, and I asked her if Sarah's leg was better. Her mom looked very surprised, and then she told me that she didn't know what I was talking about. She said that Sarah had never hurt her leg.

It was then that I realized that Sarah had stayed with me at my birthday party just to make me feel better. My true friend, Sarah, gave me the best present of all.

—Ashley Russell, 10

5 Ways to Spread Sunshine . . . with a Smile!

1. Start your own "smile" box. Write jokes or draw funny pictures on pieces of paper, fold them up, and add them to your new box. Any time you feel like you need cheering up, pick one out at random.

2. Ask friends or family if you can practice jokes or share new joke ideas with them. It might give you inspiration and them a good laugh.

3. Help a friend if they look worried or sad. Tell them things you think they're good at and why they're super cool.

4. If you can't meet with someone you know, phone them and brighten their day. (You might need a parent or caregiver's permission or help.)

5. Form your own Sunshine Squad of everyday heroes. Ask friends to join, and think of ways to spread sunshine in your neighborhood. What is your superpower? Say it proud, and with a big smile!

Published by Charlesbridge
9 Galen Street
Watertown, MA 02472
(617) 926-0329
www.charlesbridge.com

Library of Congress Cataloging-in-Publication Data
Names: LaRocca, Rajani, author. | Valle, India, illustrator.
Title: Chicken soup for the soul kids: Lucas's tricky day: looking on the bright side /
    Rajani LaRocca; illustrated by India Valle.
Description: Watertown, MA: Charlesbridge Publishing, [2022] | Series:
    Chicken Soup for the Soul KIDS | Audience: Ages 4–7. | Audience: Grades
    K–1. | Summary: "Lucas is usually quick with a joke to cheer everyone up,
    but he is feeling down because his friend Henry cannot come to his sleepover.
    The Sunshine Squad pals do their best to assure him that friends can give you
    a boost to look on the bright side."—Provided by publisher.
Identifiers: LCCN 2021039527 (print) | LCCN 2021039528 (ebook) |
    ISBN 9781623542832 (hardcover) | ISBN 9781632899545 (ebook)
Subjects: LCSH: Cheerfulness—Juvenile fiction. | Friendship—Juvenile
    fiction. | CYAC: Cheerfulness—Fiction. | Friendship—Fiction.
Classification: LCC PZ7.1.L353 Lu 2022 (print) | LCC PZ7.1.L353 (ebook) |
    DDC [E]—dc23
LC record available at https://lccn.loc.gov/2021039527
LC ebook record available at https://lccn.loc.gov/2021039528

Printed in China
(hc) 10 9 8 7 6 5 4 3 2 1

Illustrations created digitally
Display type set in Midnight Chalker by Hanoded
Text type set in Oxford by Roger White
Printed by 1010 Printing International Limited
in Huizhou, Guangdong, China
Production supervision by Jennifer Most Delaney
Designed by Kristen Nobles